A Trailblazer Curriculum Guide

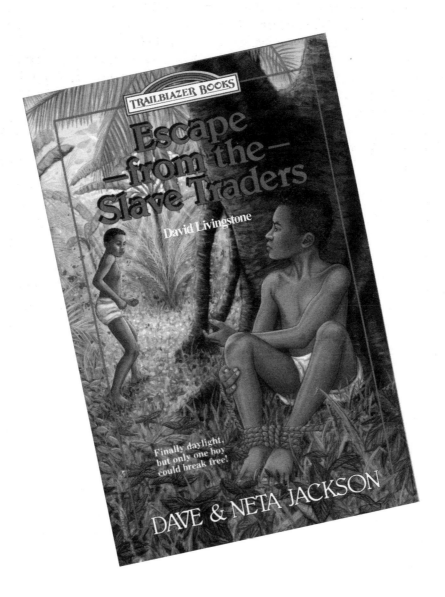

JULIA PFERDEHIRT

WITH DAVE & NETA JACKSON

BETHANY HOUSE PUBLISHERS
MINNEAPOLIS, MINNESOTA 55438

CONTENTS

Copyright © 2000
Julia Pferdehirt with Dave and Neta Jackson

Illustrations © 2000
Bethany House Publishers

Published by Bethany House Publishers
A Ministry of Bethany Fellowship International
11400 Hampshire Ave. South
Minneapolis, Minnesota 55438
www.bethanyhouse.com
ISBN 0-7642-2346-1
Printed in the United States of America by
Bethany Press International, Minneapolis, Minnesota 55438

HOW TO USE THIS GUIDE

Welcome to the TRAILBLAZER BOOKS Curriculum Guides! As a teacher or homeschooling parent, you're glad when you see your students with their noses in books. But a good story is only the beginning of a learning adventure. Since the TRAILBLAZER BOOKS take readers all over the world into different cultures and time periods, each book opens a door to an exciting, humanities-based study that includes geography, history, social studies, literature, and language arts.

This Curriculum Guide for *Escape From the Slave Traders* about David Livingstone puts a host of activities and resources at your fingertips to help launch your students on a journey of discovery. The wealth of options allows you to choose the best pace and content for your students. You might want to assign students to simply read the book and then do one or two projects on folklore or food, travel or topography. Or you can delve deeper, planning a two-week unit with daily reading and vocabulary, research, creative writing, and hands-on projects. *Advance planning is key to effective use of this guide.*

SCOPE AND SEQUENCE

This guide includes **seven lessons**, enough for a two-week unit. The first and last lessons cover one chapter; all other lessons cover two chapters. All lessons include vocabulary, background information, discussion questions, and suggested activities. **Activities** are grouped by subject matter in the back of this guide: Geography (GEO), History (HIS), Social Studies and Folkways (SS/FW), and Literature and Language Arts (LIT/LA). Within each subject, look for symbols indicating different types of activities (writing, research, speech, reading, hands-on projects, video). Activities and resources particularly appropriate for younger or older students are designated as follows: younger (*), older (**). A three- to five-day Mega Project is also included. All activities list resources and materials needed.

PLANNING

Four to six weeks prior to the study . . .

- Skim *Escape From the Slave Traders*, review lessons (pages 4–10), and choose activities, noting materials needed.

- Reserve materials on interlibrary loan and order films from specialty sources. (Titles and authors are listed in the **Activities** sections; full publication information is available under **Resources** on page 23 of this guide.)
- Purchase craft materials.

If you are planning a two-week unit . . .

- Students will cover one lesson daily for seven days.
- Choose one or more short, focused activities to accompany each lesson. Activities especially appropriate to the chapter(s) covered are noted on each lesson page.
- The remaining days can be devoted to the **Mega Project** found on page 17.

Note: Choose activities based on the age level, interests, and learning needs of your student(s). You might choose one activity from each discipline during the unit, *or* you might opt to balance the different types of activities.

LESSONS

- Assign relevant chapters in *Escape From the Slave Traders* the day before the lesson, to be read either individually *or* out loud.
- **Praise and Prayer**, written by TRAILBLAZER authors Dave and Neta Jackson, provides an opportunity for students to spend a short time in God's Word and apply scriptural concepts to their own lives.
- Read aloud the **Background** segment, then discuss **Vocabulary and Concepts**. (*Or* ask students to use context clues and a dictionary to define unfamiliar words as they read, leaving puzzling words or concepts to discuss the following day.)
- Give students an opportunity to discuss thoughts and reactions to their reading using the questions in the **Talk About It** feature. Discussion, debate, and interaction can be lively. Enjoy!
- Use the suggested **Activities**, or one of your own choosing.

Note: Unless marked otherwise, page and chapter numbers refer to Dave and Neta Jackson's original TRAILBLAZER BOOK *Escape From the Slave Traders*.

HISTORICAL SUMMARY

David Livingstone, doctor, missionary, explorer, and fighter in the struggle to end slavery, was an adventurer who laid the foundation for missionary work in central Africa where the name of Jesus had never been heard.

Born in Scotland in 1813, David Livingstone worked six-day weeks in a textile mill. He studied English and Latin and, through hard work and prayer, became a doctor. In 1841 he arrived in Cape Town, South Africa, as a medical missionary.

At that time most African countries were *colonies* "owned" and governed by Holland, France, Belgium, Germany, Italy, Portugal, Spain, or England. A colony was like a river pumped dry. Many rulers did not care what happened to a colony's people, culture, or economy as long as the rulers themselves became wealthy. Europeans controlled Africa's trade, government, education, and industry. Although Africa had great wealth in rubber, minerals, gold, and diamonds, Europeans took that, too.

In Zaire, Belgium's King Leopold once forced each village to send four workers to rubber plantations each year. At best, this was slavery. At worst, the men were worked to death. And if they refused, whole villages were massacred.

Europeans and Arabs made money in Africa another way—by kidnapping or buying slaves. From western Africa in particular, hundreds of thousands of people were ripped from their villages and families, crammed aboard European slave ships, and sold as slaves in America and Arab nations.

David Livingstone found that governments were not the only ones treating African people badly. Many missionaries never stepped off their comfortable estates. Some missionaries questioned whether Africans had souls! At best, they treated Africans like unintelligent children.

Not David Livingstone! He fought the slave trade, learned African languages, and explored inland Africa to reach people who had never heard of Jesus. He continued to explore new territory for missions even when he had to support his work by writing books about his travels and adventures!

Lesson One

CHAPTER 1: RED CAPS IN THE MIST

PRAISE AND PRAYER: THE SECOND GREAT COMMANDMENT

What we often call the Golden Rule, "Do unto others as you would have them do unto you," makes clear Jesus' teaching. **Read Matthew 7:12 and Mark 12:28–31.** How would you like to give up your freedom and belong to someone else, working without pay all day, every day, for that person, with no opportunity to make your own life decisions? That's what slavery entailed, not to mention the cruelty that usually accompanied it.

Thought: No one who values his own freedom could own slaves or support slavery and still obey the Golden Rule.

Prayer: Thank you, Lord, for my freedom, and help me always to respect and support the freedom of others.

> Wikatani looked as if he were fighting for his life!

VOCABULARY AND CONCEPTS

yam, feuded
What is a "thatched roof" (p. 18)?

BACKGROUND

Slavery is a part of Africa's history. On Africa's west coast, powerful tribes sold their less-powerful neighbors to European slave traders. In war, winners would sell the losers as slaves. Slave traders from England, Spain, Portugal, Holland, France, and other European countries took Africans by ship across the Atlantic Ocean to the Americas. Some African people were sold as slaves on sugar plantations in Jamaica, Cuba, or the Dominican Republic. Others were enslaved in the United States, leaving a shameful scar on America's history.

On Africa's east coast, kidnapped Africans were sold to Arab slave traders. Sometimes organized groups, like the Red Caps mentioned in *Escape From the Slave Traders*, would trick tribes into fighting, then sell the losers to the Arabs.

Arab slave traders became wealthy selling slaves not only in Arabia, but also to other traders who brought them to the New World. According to *People in Bondage* by L. H. Ofosu, Arabs bought and sold African slaves until 1964!

TALK ABOUT IT

When God tells us *not* to do something, He has a reason—even if we don't understand it. Slavery is wrong for many reasons. List at least three. Share and discuss. (*Note:* Some students will suggest slavery is wrong because "God said so" or "it's mean." Encourage deeper thinking. For example, slavery denies God-given free will. Slavery treats humans [God's image] like animals. A tree is known by its fruit; slavery's fruit was cruelty, broken families, etc.)

ACTIVITIES

GEO 1; HIS 1, 2, 3; LIT/LA 1

Lesson Two

CHAPTER 2: **WAR DRUMS**
CHAPTER 3: **IN CAMP WITH THE "ENEMY"**

PRAISE AND PRAYER: WHO IS UNABLE TO LOVE GOD?

According to **Matthew 25:40 and 45**, how we relate to the helpless people around us is how we treat Jesus. But the Bible even goes further and says that some people are even unable to love God. **Read 1 John 4:16–21**.

Thought: Because human beings were created in the image of God (Genesis 1:26), everyone deserves basic respect.

Prayer: Thank you, Lord, for loving and creating me in your image. Help me to realize that how I treat others is how I treat you.

VOCABULARY AND CONCEPTS

groping, skeptically
What is a "smoldering fire" on page 20?
What does "gigantic smoking canoes" on page 37 mean?

BACKGROUND

The trick played on the Ajawa and Manganja tribes was played on others. If one tribe could be convinced to attack another, the slave traders had only to wait until the battle was over and buy the losers! Sometimes traders hired strong men from the "winning" tribe to herd the captives to waiting slave ships. Then everyone—winners and losers alike—was sold to the slave traders.

By 1841, when David Livingstone arrived in Africa, Portugal was the leading slave-trading nation, providing slaves for the sugarcane plantations in Brazil and Cuba. The sugar, which was grown, harvested, and processed by slaves, was made into molasses. Slave ships brought new slaves, then picked up loads of molasses. In the United States, the molasses was made into rum. The rum was then taken to Africa and traded for more slaves. This trade route—from Africa to Brazil and Cuba, then to the U.S., then back to Africa—became known as the "rum route."

By 1841, U.S. law didn't allow new slaves to be brought from Africa, but slave traders continued to do this illegally.

When the girl looked their way, Chuma motioned to her to come over to them.

TALK ABOUT IT

Sojourner Truth, a Christian evangelist, speaker, and former slave, once said slaves might lose their freedom and their lives, but slave owners were in greater danger—they could lose their souls.

How do you think owning slaves might change a person's character? If a slave owner treated slaves well, would the result be the same? Why or why not?

ACTIVITIES

GEO 2, 3; HIS 5, 6, 7; SS/FW 1

Lesson Three

PRAISE AND PRAYER: DEVELOPING TRUSTWORTHINESS

Why do we mistrust people? Usually it is because they or other people have proven untrustworthy in the past. **Read Luke 16:10–13.** Jesus teaches the principle of developing our trustworthiness by being faithful in the small things so that we can be trusted with greater things in his kingdom.

Thought: Sometimes we want a big, glamorous role before we have learned how to be trustworthy in something small.

Prayer: Lord, thank you for the little tasks that you give me. Help me learn to do them well so you can give me more important things to do for you.

VOCABULARY AND CONCEPTS

caravan
What does "trilling their grief" on page 40 mean?

BACKGROUND

In the 1840s, Africans like Chuma and Wikatani may have seen few white people or even none. David Livingstone left the cities and mission compounds where most missionaries spent all their time, and traveled inland to find tribes and settlements where no one had heard of Jesus.

In Livingstone's time, most of Africa was unknown to white Europeans. Coastal cities and some rivers were charted on maps, but inland Africa was mostly unmapped and unexplored by white people.

TALK ABOUT IT

On page 54, we read that Wikatani and Chuma saw the white man pour something into a cup for a sick child. Chuma thought the white man looked kind and trustworthy, but Wikatani said, *"Wait…maybe he poisoned the child. You saw how he laughed. It's better to stay hidden…until we are sure."* Wikatani and Chuma each saw the same thing. Yet one felt trusting and the other didn't.

Talk about times when you and others have shared the same experience but felt and understood it differently. What influenced your reactions? Why do people sometimes interpret situations wrongly? What can you do when you realize you've been wrong? How can you keep from making wrong assumptions again?

Example: Imagine you and your friends are raising money for a homeless shelter. Your mom offers to handle the money. One friend says your mom is nice to help. Another friend complains that adults always think kids can't handle money.

ACTIVITIES

GEO 3; HIS 8; SS/FW 2, 3; LIT/LA 2

This bound each pair of men together as though there were just one pole between them.

Lesson Four

CHAPTER 6: "LIVINGSTONE'S CHILDREN"
CHAPTER 7: A DESPERATE PLAN

PRAISE AND PRAYER: SPEAKING OUT AGAINST INJUSTICE

God hates injustice, especially when it oppresses the helpless. **Read Proverbs 31:8–9 and Jeremiah 5:26–29.** God doesn't care more for poor people than for rich people (Acts 10:34–35). However, rich people usually have ways of helping themselves, while the poor do not.

Thought: Jesus once said, "He who is not with me is against me" (Matthew 12:30). Could the same be true of the poor? If we do not speak up for them, does God count us as against them? Are we in danger of God's punishment?

Prayer: Give me a heart of love for those in need and the courage to speak up on their behalf.

VOCABULARY AND CONCEPTS

machetes, brashness, silhouetting

What does Dr. Livingstone mean when he says the Red Caps "use my good name to gain access into tribes that were once safe from all outsiders"?

BACKGROUND

The Red Caps worked for Portuguese slave traders. Portugal and England had signed a treaty forbidding slave trade, so when Dr. Livingstone discovered Portuguese merchants buying and selling slaves with their government's permission, he told British church and government officials.

But Britain did nothing. Britain valued trade with Portugal more than ending slavery. Dr. Livingstone was ordered to be quiet. Instead, he kept writing letters and even returned to England to tell the truth. He kept speaking out even when the British government took away his "charter" (official permission) as a missionary!

TALK ABOUT IT

When Chuma and Wikatani called a steamboat a "smoking canoe," they compared a new and unknown sight to something familiar. In the same way, airplanes have been called "silver birds" or cars called "horseless carriages."

Recall when you first saw something new or strange. What did you think? How did you figure out what it was or how it worked? Were your guesses correct? Did you feel excited? Confused? Uninformed?

(*Note:* Recall when you first saw a palm-sized computer. Did you think it was a calculator? What did you do? This was cutting-edge technology in a machine the size of a paperback book! How did you feel?)

ACTIVITIES

GEO 4, 5, 6; HIS 9, 10, 11, 12; SS/FW 4; LIT/LA 3

Finally the doctor noticed the boy behind him and turned. "What's the matter, son?"

Lesson Five

PRAISE AND PRAYER: TESTING FOR THE TRUTH

Read 1 John 4:1–6 and discover how we can tell the difference between truth and falsehood. This does not mean that everything a Christian says is true and everything an unbeliever says is false (even the devil quoted true Scriptures when trying to tempt Jesus). But the devil's ultimate purpose is to mislead us because he is a liar and the father of lies (John 8:44).

Thought: The first step in recognizing truth from falsehood involves inviting God to cleanse our hearts of all falsehood.

Prayer: "Search me, O God, and know my heart; test me and know my anxious thoughts. See if there is any offensive way in me" (Psalm 139:23–24, NIV).

VOCABULARY AND CONCEPTS

ambush, whiffed, brambles, flotilla, dejected, cataract

Why does the Manganja warrior call the Ajawa "treacherous hyenas" on page 86?

What does "turbulent" rapids on page 91 mean?

Wikatani scrambled onto the ant hill, stood up, and yelled, "Don't shoot! Don't shoot!"

BACKGROUND

Even when Dr. Livingstone had a map of an area, such maps often included only basic information. Sometimes white explorers followed and mapped a river or lake, but anything beyond the shore was still unknown. African people carried maps in their minds, so if a white explorer asked about the surrounding land, he might be told only about places important to that person or tribe.

So it was not surprising that Dr. Livingstone's map of the river didn't show how dangerous the Murchison cataracts were.

TALK ABOUT IT

The Red Caps used deception and rumors to get the Manganja and Ajawa tribes to fight. They kidnapped the boys and made it look like the work of the Manganja. An untrue rumor then flew through the Ajawa villages that the Manganja had broken the peace. The Ajawa believed the lie and the rumor and attacked their Manganja neighbors.

Have you ever believed a rumor that turned out to be untrue? What did you do? What happened? How can you find out if rumors are true?

ACTIVITIES

GEO 7, 8, 9, 10; LIT/LA 6, 7, 8; CT 1, 2

Lesson Six

CHAPTER 10: THE SECOND JOURNEY
CHAPTER 11: LAKE NYASSA

PRAISE AND PRAYER: TAKING THE LONG VIEW

In this microwave world we want instant results: hot meals within three minutes, entertainment at the press of a button, and rewards on the spot for doing what God wants us to do. **Read 1 Corinthians 3:6–15.** You will see that Paul encouraged a longer-term view. He realized that preaching the Gospel or encouraging someone might not have an immediate result. But God would ultimately reward us for doing right.

Thought: If our only reason for being kind to other people is so they will like us, we might be disappointed.

Prayer: Lord, help me do what is right always, not because other people will respond positively, but because it pleases you.

VOCABULARY AND CONCEPTS

hoisted, interior, portaging, toil
What does "faces etched with concern" on page 96 mean?
What does "I must not be shortsighted" mean on page 104?

BACKGROUND

The dangers Dr. Livingstone faced are amazing. Traveling in uncharted areas where weather was unpredictable and the animals deadly, Livingstone and others risked their lives. An overturned boat or broken bone could mean death.

Dr. Livingstone used the experience gained in these expeditions to support his ministry later. When the English government took away his missionary charter because of his public protests against the slave trade, Dr. Livingstone began writing about his adventures in Africa. Income from these books provided money for more exploration and opening of new territories for missions.

TALK ABOUT IT

Dr. Livingstone wasted no time telling about Jesus. As soon as he could communicate, he began to tell each tribe about the God who created everything and his Son, Jesus. Why did Dr. Livingstone bother to talk about something people could barely understand? Do you think this was a good idea? What did he mean by *"I planted a seed"* on page 107?

Missionaries often plant seeds knowing they will not be around to see if anything "grows." Describe one way you have planted a seed. What happened?

ACTIVITIES

GEO 11, 12, 13, 14; HIS 13, 14; LIT/LA 9, 10; CT 3

Porters carried a rowboat as they headed north. Two men went ahead and cleared the way with machetes.

Lesson Seven

CHAPTER 12: HOME AND BEYOND
CHAPTER 13: EPILOGUE
MORE ABOUT DAVID LIVINGSTONE

PRAISE AND PRAYER: BEING A LIVING SACRIFICE

To lay down one's life so someone else can live is the supreme sacrifice. Jesus did this for us, and he asks us to follow him in giving our lives for others. But more often we are asked to *live* in service and ministry for others rather than *die*. **Read Romans 12:1–2 and 14:7–8.**

Thought: Sometimes we may hope or even imagine that we could bravely die for Christ if put to the test, but we forget how we are put to the test to *live* for him by serving those around us with simple deeds of kindness every day.

Prayer: Dear Lord, grant me the patience, the courage, and the dedication to serve others as though I were serving you.

VOCABULARY AND CONCEPTS

elated, craggy, thatched, ambushed, conjecture
What does "laughed wryly" on page 117 mean?
What does "that fateful day" on page 126 mean?

"You know, Chuma, you could come with me," said Dr. Livingstone.

BACKGROUND

David Livingstone "gave away" his life for Christ, even when he didn't seem to get much in return. He lost friendships and the support of his mission board because of his protests against slavery. He spent years exploring and befriending tribes in hopes that mission work would develop, but he rarely saw that work bloom and grow. He told people about Jesus and moved on, often without knowing if the seeds he'd planted would bring people to salvation. Sadly, he died before the slave trade ended in central Africa.

Some people considered David Livingstone a failure. Others thought he was simply peculiar because he began churches, trained African leaders, and moved on to share about Jesus in a new place. David Livingstone is an example of someone who worked faithfully, following God's call.

TALK ABOUT IT

On the long trip to their village with Dr. Livingstone, Chuma and Wikatani each *thought* about their fears that the Manganja warriors had destroyed their home, but they didn't talk about them. Tell about a time when you've been worried but didn't want to talk about it. Why did you choose not to talk? Would you choose the same way again?

ACTIVITIES

HIS 15, 16

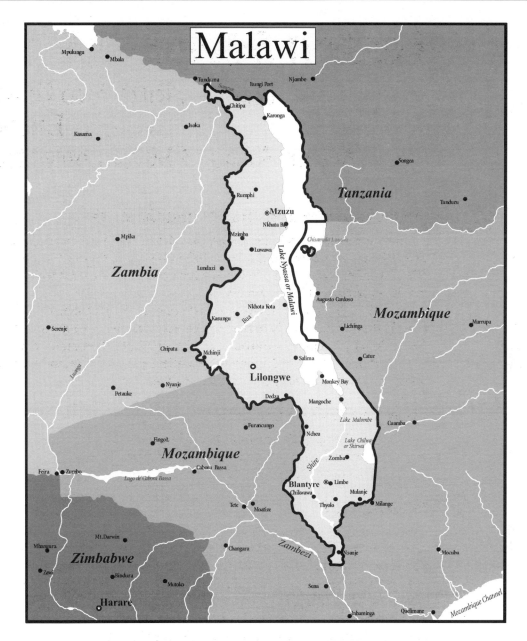

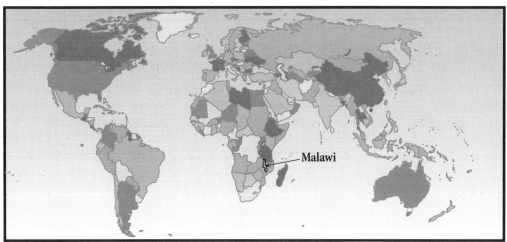

Escape From the Slave Traders

Geography

If we know the land, we will know more about the people. In a land like Africa, bordered by ocean and containing mountains, savanna, jungle, and desert, the land determines much about how people live.

As advances in technology (television, Internet, etc.) make our world smaller and smaller, students must know about other countries. To understand the news and politics, students need to understand how and where people live around the world. So geography is more than finding Africa on a map; it includes understanding how the land affects people and culture.

 GEO 1: Trace a map of Africa, including national boundaries, major rivers, and lakes. Use a color code to mark jungle (rain forest), desert, and mountain areas. Mark Malawi, Mozambique, Lake Nyassa, Lake Shirwa, the Shire River, and the Zambezi River. (HANDS-ON)

 GEO 2: Trace the "rum route" of slave traders on a map. Information about this is available in encyclopedias and in *People in Bondage* by L. H. Ofosu. (HANDS-ON)

 GEO 3: Even if captured Africans managed to escape slave traders, it was difficult to return home. Some tribes were *nomadic*, moving from place to place. Others never traveled more than a hundred or so miles from their villages. How would someone find a small village hundreds of miles away through unfamiliar territory?

See GEO 1 above. When you have completed the map for this activity, search online or print encyclopedias or books on African history and culture for maps showing tribal territories. Add tribal names and territories to your map. (HANDS-ON)

 GEO 4: Many Westerners still wrongly think all Africans are brown-skinned and live in rain forests. To understand the "real" diversity of Africa, trace a map of Africa on a *large* sheet of poster board. (If a map was created for GEO 1, you may wish to use this.) Label the countries' current names. Search for photos of African people, places, and traditional dress from as many countries as you can find. Good sources include travel and cultural/history publications like *National Geographic, Travel,* or *Faces*; Web sites like http://dpsnet.detpub.k12.mi.us/heritage/gallery.htm; photocopies of pictures in library books or magazines.

Cut and glue photos around your map like a picture frame. Link photos with the correct country using drawn lines, string, or color-coded pushpins. The result will be colorful, beautiful images of Africa and its people.

(*Note:* Garage sales are sometimes good sources for back issues of *National Geographic* and other travel publications. Or try asking for old issues by placing an ad in a local paper, church bulletin, or public posting board at the library or grocery. Some homeschoolers even carry two subscriptions to *National Geographic*—one for the family library and another to provide photos for school projects.) (HANDS-ON)

 GEO 5: The characters in *Escape From the Slave Traders* traveled at the edge of the central African rain forest. Dense rain forest allowed tribes like the Manganja and Ajawa to remain isolated and separate from others. Learn about the rain forest and the people who live there. Good resources include *A Walk Through a Rain Forest* by David and Mark Jenike and Web sites like www.passporttoknowledge.com/rainforest (both geosystem and ecosystem sections). (RESEARCH)

GEO 6: Trek the rain forest and down the Congo River at www.nationalgeographic.com/congotrek/. This Web site includes correspondence with Michael Fay, a National Geographic Society scientist hoping to record life in the central African rain forest now, before human presence in the form of industry, development, or vacation resorts destroys more forest. (INTERNET)

GEO 7: Where is Dr. Livingstone's group? Find the Shire River, Mount Zomba, and the south shore of Lake Shirwa on a map. (HANDS-ON)

GEO 8: Find the Murchison cataracts on a map (see page 89 for a description of their location). If you have been creating a map of Dr. Livingstone's journey, add the cataracts to your map. (HANDS-ON)

GEO 9: View the video *Journey to 1,000 Rivers*. This is the story of Jacques Cousteau's eighteen-month expedition down a rain forest river, the Amazon. It is worth seeing because of the similarity to the environment of Africa's rain forest and rivers. (VIDEO)

GEO 10: View the National Geographic Video *World's Greatest Places: Hidden Congo.* (VIDEO)

GEO 11: Dr. Livingstone mapped unexplored places. Your library may have United States Geological Survey maps. Examine one to find out how differences in elevation are shown. How would you know whether a mountain hike would be steep or gradual?

Find plat maps at your city hall or historical society. These micro-maps show neighborhoods.

Find your own house or lot on a plat map.

A map that includes every lane and stream and country road is called a *gazetteer*. Compare a gazetteer to a normal atlas-type road map. (RESEARCH)

GEO 12: Use your Internet browser to find maps from various Web sites. Or try www.expediamaps.com.

First find a map of your own community. "Plan" a trip by typing in your home (say, Kalamazoo, Michigan) and destination (say, 1600 Pennsylvania Avenue, Washington, D.C.). The computer will generate a map for this trip. Click to the World Maps section and request a map of locations in *Escape From the Slave Traders* like Lake Nyassa, the Zambezi River, or Lake Shirwa. (INTERNET)

GEO 13: View old and even ancient maps of Africa at www.raremaps.com (see Africa). Search the Internet for old maps using the search words *maps + ancient* or *cartography*. (INTERNET)

GEO 14: A map of the expedition to Lake Nyassa is on page 8 of *Escape From the Slave Traders.* Trace the journey on a map of Malawi. How long was their trek up the Shire River to reach Lake Nyassa at the southern end? (HANDS-ON)

GEO 15: Find the Zambezi river on a map. The Red Caps planned to sell Chuma, Wikatani, and the others to Arab traders who shipped people down the Zambezi to slave stations on the coast. Today, paths worn deep in the earth by the feet of thousands of people forced to walk into slavery can still be found in this area! (HANDS-ON)

History

An old saying claims that people who don't know history are doomed to repeat it. Whether that is true or not, knowing history helps us to understand why people behave as they do, how governments work, and how one event causes another as history unfolds.

 HIS 1: Read about the history of the slave trade in *People in Bondage* by L. H. Ofosu, *Middle Passage* by Tom Feelings, or *From Slave Ship to Freedom Road* by Julius Lester. (READING)

 HIS 2: Learn about the "rum route" of slave trade. See chapter 3 of *People in Bondage* by L. H. Ofosu or the July 1984 and September 1992 issues of *National Geographic* magazine. Online and print encyclopedias include information, as well. (RESEARCH)

 HIS 3: Read about David Livingstone's entire life and ministry in *Africa's Trailblazer* by Janet and Geoff Benge. (READING)

 HIS 4: Read a *fictional* book about people brought from Africa to slavery and present a "book talk" to your family, class, or homeschool group. Book talks are brief five- to ten-sentence summaries of a book and its main character. Include at least three reasons why you recommend or don't recommend this book.

Some good titles include *The Slave Dancer* by Paula Fox, *The Runaway's Revenge* by Dave and Neta Jackson, *My Name Is not Angelica* by Scott O'Dell, and *The Captive* by Joyce Hansen. (READING)

 HIS 5: **Kidnapped Africans did not go willingly to slavery! Read about the slave ship mutiny on the *Amistad* in *Freedom's Sons: The True Story of the Amistad Mutiny* by Suzanne Jurmain or *Amistad: A Long Road to Freedom* by Walter Dean Myers. (These books are inappropriate for younger students.) (READING)

 HIS 6: **Older students may watch the video *Amistad*, available at most rental outlets and libraries. This difficult, sometimes violent video includes a fascinating segment in which enslaved people, on trial for their lives and freedom, discover the Bible and identify with Jesus. (*Note:* This video *must* be previewed for age-appropriate content.) (VIDEO)

 HIS 7: Learn about early African history in *African Beginnings* by James Haskins and Kathleen Benson. Follow the history by noting events, people, and places on a timeline. (RESEARCH)

 HIS 8: Malawi was just one of the African countries where David Livingstone fought slavery. Learn about slave trade in Malawi. One source is the book *Malawi* by Martha S. B. Lane. Chapter 3 tells about Livingstone's attempts to end slavery. (This book is out of print but is available on interlibrary loan.) (READING)

 HIS 9: Bishop Mackenzie was a real missionary. Learn more about him at www.trailblazerbooks.com. Click on the cover icon for *Escape From the Slave Traders* and choose "Web Links." (INTERNET)

*Mega Project for Younger Students

 HIS 10: Learn all you can about slavery in the United States using books, magazines, and the Internet. Write a report telling about the lives and experiences of people in slavery.

Find this history in *Many Thousand Gone* by Virginia Hamilton.

Read slaves' stories in their own words in *Our Song, Our Toil* by Michele Stepto or use the Internet at www.loc.gov/exhibits/african/ (click on "Slave Narratives").

Read about slavery in the July 1984 issue of *National Geographic* magazine or find this article on the Internet at www.nationalgeographic.com/features/99/railroad. (MEGA)

**Mega Project for Older Students

 HIS 11: The slave trade David Livingstone fought so hard to end became part of American history, as well. People of African heritage were trapped in slavery in the United States for nearly 250 years.

For this activity, learn all you can about slavery in this country:
- Create a timeline.
- Include a map of the "rum route" of the slave traders.
- Read at least one "slave narrative," a first-person story of a slave's own life.
- Read one fictional book about slavery.
- Finally, choose a topic about slavery to research and write about.

Other Mega Project information sources not listed above:
Online:
> http://odur.let.rug.nl/~usa/D/1826-1850/slavery/fugit06
> http://memory.loc.gov/ammem/ (search for African odyssey, timeline, photos)
> http://scriptorium.lib.duke.edu/campbell/ (slave narratives, links to many other good sites)

Print:
> *The Underground Railroad* by Charles Blockson
> *Get on Board: The Story of the Underground Railroad* by Jim Haskins
> ***From Slave Ship to Freedom Road* by Julius Lester (appropriate for older students only)
> *Incidents in the Life of a Slave Girl* by Harriet Jacobs
> *Escape From Slavery: The Boyhood of*

> *Frederick Douglass in His Own Words* edited by Michael McCurdy
> *The Refugees: Narratives of Fugitive Slaves in Canada* by Benjamin Drew (This book is out of print. Try interlibrary loan.)

Other Mega Project Ideas:
Tell about the daily lives, families, work, housing, and experiences of people in slavery.

Create an exhibit by reading at least five slave narratives from sources listed above and writing a summary of each person's experience. Include a map of each escape route, if possible. Copy photos if available.

Research the history of slavery or the Underground Railroad in your own state. Write what you learn in a report to share with others.

Learn and write a report about one of the following American freedom fighters:
> Thomas Garrett (See *Dear Friend* by Judith Bentley)
> Levi and Catherine Coffin (See *Reminiscences of Levi Coffin*)
> Harriet Tubman (See *Listen for the Whippoorwill* by Dave and Neta Jackson and *Get on Board* by Jim Haskins)
> William Still (See *One Day, Levin...He Be Free* by Lurey Khan and other books by William Still)
> Frederick Douglass (See *Escape From Slavery* above)
> Lucretia Mott
> Harriet Beecher Stowe (See *Harriet Beecher Stowe and the Beecher Preachers* by Jean Fritz)
> Jermaine Loguen
> Henry "Box" Brown (See *Many Thousand Gone* by Virginia Hamilton)
> William and Ellen Craft (See *Escape From Slavery: Five Journeys to Freedom* by Doreen Rappaport)
> John Brown
> Eliza Harris (See *Many Thousand Gone* by Virginia Hamilton)
> Sojourner Truth (See *Walking the Road to Freedom* by Jeri Ferris)
> Elijah Lovejoy
> Dred Scott
(MEGA)

HIS 12: Travel the Underground Railroad today with Tony Cohen. This scholar, historian, and great-great-grandson of slaves traced the route taken by his own ancestor fleeing to Canada. He has since walked other escape routes. Read about Tony's journeys at www.ugrr.org/ugrr or in the July 1996 issue of *Smithsonian* magazine. (INTERNET)

 HIS 13: Dr. Livingstone did lose his entire supply of medicine in a boating accident. Read about it at www.trailblazerbooks.com. Click on the *Escape From the Slave Traders* book cover to learn more about Dr. Livingstone's life. (INTERNET)

 HIS 14: To see drawings of David Livingstone, read from his journal, and learn about Henry Stanley, the reporter who found Livingstone in central Africa, go to www.sc.edu/library/spcoll/sccoll/africa/africa5.html. (INTERNET)

 HIS 15: Learn more about David Livingstone's life at the Web sites listed in HIS 13 and 14. Another good source is *Africa's Trailblazer* by Janet and Geoff Benge. (RESEARCH)

 HIS 16: Learn about the famous meeting between Henry Stanley and Dr. Livingstone. Mr. Stanley, a reporter for the *New York Herald* newspaper, was sent to find Dr. Livingstone. Many people thought Dr. Livingstone had died in central Africa. In addition to the Web site listed in HIS 14, online and print encyclopedias also include this story. Your library will have books covering the event, as well.

Write a summary of the journey taken by Henry Stanley. Your state historical society or university library may have microvideo copies of the old newspapers carrying Mr. Stanley's amazing adventure story of his journey and of finding Dr. Livingstone, still at work, in the heart of Africa. (WRITING)

Social Studies and Folkways

Folkways are the traditions of a people and culture. Art, foods, storytelling, music, dance, drama, literature, and even religion reflect the heart and soul of a nation and its people.

For Western people, understanding African culture, values, and traditions is especially challenging. Our cultures are very, very different. Yet, as David Livingstone discovered, when we share the traditions of our neighbors, they become friends.

 SS/FW 1: Ask your librarian for a tape or CD of traditional African songs or drumming.

Drumming was used as entertainment and communication. In the U.S., slave owners soon realized that enslaved people could communicate with drums, so drumming and speaking African languages were forbidden. (HANDS-ON)

 SS/FW 2: See the drawing on page 44 (or page 6 of this guide). The wooden Y-shaped yokes were called *golis.* To understand how the goli worked, construct one. You'll need to find a forked stick about as big around as your arm. Choose only fallen limbs.

Place the arms of the Y-shaped goli over your shoulder so the main "leg" of the Y faces away from you. Slavers tied a straight stick to that leg to make it long and cumbersome. Sometimes two people were yoked together as shown on page 44.

If you have a partner, try lashing your yokes together in this manner. Try walking together. Try climbing steps or a hill. To share the experience of Wikatani and Chuma, try walking through tall grass in a prairie or field. (HANDS-ON)

 SS/FW 3: A common food, *nsima,* is mentioned in chapter 4. Nsima is a cornmeal mush sometimes served with a spicy sauce called *ndiwo*. Prepare a meal David Livingstone might have eaten in Malawi by purchasing dried or smoked fish at a local fish market, baking sweet potatoes, and preparing nsima and a sweet salad of citrus fruit and bananas.

Both nsima and baked sweet potatoes or yams are delicious with salt, pepper, and butter or sweetened with butter and brown sugar. (COOKING)

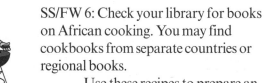 **SS/FW 4:** See GEO 4, which will help you understand the diverse people groups of Africa. (HANDS-ON)

SS/FW 5: Try this simplified recipe for West African Groundnut Stew. Ingredients: 5 tablespoons oil, divided; 2 pounds beef, cubed and rolled lightly in flour; $1/2$ teaspoon nutmeg; 1 tablespoon chili powder; 4 medium-sized onions, sliced; 1 garlic clove, minced; $3/4$ cup tomato paste; 6 cups water; red pepper if desired; $1/2$ cup chunky peanut butter; rice; chopped peanuts.

Heat 3 tablespoons oil in a heavy kettle and add the beef, nutmeg, and chili powder. When meat is browned, add onions, garlic, tomato paste, water, and red pepper. Simmer until meat is tender.

One half hour before serving, heat the peanut butter and remaining 2 tablespoons of oil for five minutes over medium heat. Stir. Add to beef stew. Simmer on low about 20 minutes.

Serve over rice and garnish with peanuts. (COOKING)

SS/FW 6: Check your library for books on African cooking. You may find cookbooks from separate countries or regional books.

Use these recipes to prepare an African supper. Serve your meal seated on the floor around a brightly-colored tablecloth. (COOKING)

SS/FW 7: Find and learn an African folktale. Your family, class, or homeschool group may want to choose folktales from different regions of Africa. Learn this folktale by reading and rereading it. Finally, tell the tale as a story-teller. Some storytellers memorize their stories word for word, while others learn the basic tale and memorize important words and phrases.

Tell your story to your family, class, or homeschool group. (SPEECH)

 SS/FW 8: The famous tales of Anansi (or Ananse) the spider come from western and central Africa. Ask your librarian to help you find an Anansi tale from Africa and one from either America or the Caribbean. How are the tales different? Similar? Read both to your family, class, or homeschool group and tell how and why you think the folktale has changed. (SPEECH)

 SS/FW 9: The Brer Rabbit stories also have African roots. The stories come from cultures where traditions were passed from person to person *orally* (in spoken words and stories) rather than in written form. These stories were told to entertain, to express ideas, or even to teach morals. In slavery, people used the stories for another reason—to give information their white slave masters did not understand. Read some Brer Rabbit stories aloud. Talk about how they entertain, express ideas, or teach morals. (SPEECH)

 SS/FW 10: *Be a Friend: The Story of African American Music in Song, Words, and Pictures* by Leotha Stanley tells how African music became slavery songs, which became African-American music today. This book and tape may be available from your public library, or it can be purchased from Knowledge Unlimited, Inc. at (800) 356-2303. (HANDS-ON)

 SS/FW 11: Read *The People Could Fly* by Virginia Hamilton. This folktale is interesting because, as Ms. Hamilton tells her readers, African stories about people flying are still told. Other American tellings of African folktales include *Mufaro's Beautiful Daughters* and *Why Mosquitoes Buzz in People's Ears.*

Choose one folktale—or better yet, read all three. Look for images or characteristics you think might show this story's African roots. (READING)

 SS/FW 12: Scout area import stores, specialty clothing stores, or art shops for cloth, handcrafts, and artwork from any African country. Be sure to take along a camera. Ask permission from the shop owner to take photos of these examples of African crafts. Mount your photos with a caption telling the country of origin and any other information you can learn about the items. (HANDS-0N)

 SS/FW 13: Contact area art galleries, museums, or university art departments for information about exhibits of African art in your community, county, or state. Plan a field trip to any exhibits you find. Again, photos taken (with permission—some museums do not permit photos) would make a wonderful display. (HANDS-ON)

 SS/FW 14: Sweet Honey in the Rock is the name of an a cappella singing group made up of five women singers who perform music from African roots and a sixth group member who interprets each song in American Sign Language. Some music is ancient, while other songs were created recently. These women also perform freedom songs once outlawed during apartheid in South Africa. Check your library for audio or video-tapes of this creative group. (VIDEO)

 SS/FW 15: Using photos cut from magazines and photocopies of illustra-tions and photos from books, make a poster of as many different examples of traditional African clothing as you can find. Look for the blue cloth of the Tuareg people and the Indinkra block-printed cloth of Guana. Be sure to list the country of origin beneath each picture. (HANDS-ON)

Literature and Language Arts

Stories are windows to understanding people and their culture. When we enjoy folktales or listen to song lyrics from another culture, we see and appreciate the creativity of the people.

Reading books set in another culture, like *Escape From the Slave Traders*, also makes us better writers. We see how words are used to tell a story, describe a scene, or reveal a character. Students can experiment, using those techniques in their own writing.

LIT/LA 1: Read *Africa's Trailblazer* by Janet and Geoff Benge.

After reading about David Livingstone's entire life, write an essay telling how and why Livingstone's experiences changed his character (see also HIS 3). (WRITING)

LIT/LA 2: Read *Monkey Sunday,* a story from a Congolese village, by Sanna Stanley. The Congo is north and west of Malawi, where *Escape From the Slave Traders* takes place. David Livingstone explored and lived in the Congo. (READING)

LIT/LA 3: Read the **Talk About It** section for Lesson Four of this guide. Ask your parents or grandparents to describe the first time they saw a personal computer. What did they think? What questions did they have? (Are words like *typewriter* mentioned?) (RESEARCH)

LIT/LA 4: Put yourselves in Chuma and Wikatani's place. Imagine you have never seen a steam-driven boat. Imagine you run home to tell your tribe about this amazing, fascinating, but frightening thing.

Try writing this in first person. Use the writing tool called *show, don't tell.* Don't just write, "I was by the river, and I saw a big canoe with smoke coming out of it." Instead, *show* this strange thing by describing sights, sounds, and smells. Imagine the scene. Ask yourself questions like: Did the engine roar? Did it rumble? What did the burning coal smell like? Canoes glide quietly through water; what did the moving steamboat look like? You will help your readers understand by telling your own thoughts and feelings, too. (WRITING)

LIT/LA 5: One of the most important characteristics of African literature is its roots in *oral history,* or storytelling. Some tribal groups had members (called *griots* in some western African countries) whose job was to remember and tell the tribe's history. Other tribes honored people who were gifted storytellers.

Find an African folktale or legend. Read and reread it until you either learn it word for word or know the story very well. Visit a class or group of younger children and *tell* this story.

Good storytelling requires more than just reading well. Storytellers are also actors. Try using voices, hand gestures, and facial expressions to help your story come to life.

See SS/FW 8, 9, and 11 for some book or story suggestions. Collections of folktales are other good sources. (SPEECH)

LIT/LA 6: In chapter 9, Chuma falls into the wild river.

He kicked hard as he fought for the surface, but there was no resisting the cold monster that clutched him in its grasp. Down, down he went until all was blackness, and he had no idea which way was up. Suddenly something raked the length of his back like the claws of a lion, and his head crashed into stone. He tumbled helplessly over and over. . . . The river was intent on knocking every bit of breath out of him. . . . And then the river spat him out, and he flew into the air, face up with legs and arms outstretched toward the dazzling blue sky (pages 92–93).

The authors create strong *tension* (a feeling of danger or conflict) by using a writing tool called *personification.* This means they write as if the river were a living being. Notice they call the river a "cold monster." Later, they say the river wanted to knock the breath out of Chuma's body. Finally, the river spits him out!

Imagine a dangerous setting like an avalanche, flood, blizzard, rainstorm, or dark forest. Imagine a person is lost in this danger. Write a paragraph using personification, writing as if the danger were a frightening, living thing. Write in first person, telling what the main character sees, feels, and thinks. (WRITING)

LIT/LA 7: On page 86, a Manganja warrior calls the Ajawa "treacherous hyenas." Why did the authors choose the hyena as a symbol of the man's feelings about his enemies? Saying the Ajawa were hyenas is called *metaphor.* He didn't say they were *like* hyenas; he said they *were* hyenas.

Find the metaphor here: "The man waited in the shadows behind the subway stairs. Soon, people would come pouring out of the office buildings headed for home. He waited. Patience had made him the king of thieves. He watched for a tired businessman setting his briefcase on a bench or a distracted professor with her tote bag crammed with papers and books. Then, in a second, the snake would strike and someone's fancy laptop computer would be gone."
Use a metaphor to create a word sketch of a character whom you describe as an animal. (WRITING)

LIT/LA 8: On page 90, the character Chuma says, *"If they had heard us coming and been ready, we would have been like big fish in a little pool."*
The authors use similes to show us how dangerous the situation was. Similes describe something using the words *like* or *as.*
Like big fish in a little pond means they would have been so easy to spot, the men on shore would have shot them all.

Americans have a similar expression: "It was so easy it was *like* shooting fish in a barrel!"
Create some similes of your own:
• It was as dark as . . .

• He was so angry he was like . . .
• The morning sun was like . . .
• The mountain peak rose above them like . . .
• I was as tired as . . .
• The fire flared up like . . .
• The goalie dove like . . .
• The diver stretched into the air like . . .
(WRITING)

LIT/LA 9: Imagine the scene on page 112 where *the water to the north seemed to run on into the sky.* Remember Laura Ingalls Wilder describing the prairie sky in the *Little House* books or Gary Paulsen describing the arctic snow in *Dogsong*? The TRAILBLAZER authors use descriptions of the water and sky to show us this scene.

Writers sometimes use details to create a scene. One method is to focus in on the scene like a camera, starting with the entire picture and coming closer with each sentence. Perhaps a scene set in a forest cabin might begin with descriptions of a great, rolling sea of green and brown. Branches reach like arms into the sky, trying to pull snowy clouds down to earth. (Then, like a focusing camera, the scene comes in closer.) Tree trunks are lined up like giant soldiers on the ridge. Behind them, reinforcements—entire armies of pine and oak standing guard. (Can you see the "camera" coming in still closer?)

Above a cluster of birch trees, smoke curls into the air. A log cabin squats in the clearing, its door propped open. (Come closer again.) A black mound of fur with watching blue eyes and a panting pink tongue is the only sign of life. Inside the open cabin door, the fire has turned to ash. A single empty chair stands next to the rough wooden table.

Can you imagine this scene? Can you "travel" into the scene with the writer, coming closer with every sentence?

Use this technique to describe a scene in *Escape From the Slave Traders.* You might choose a time when the expedition sights a beach on the edge of Lake Nyassa, or the moment when the group emerged from the river onto the huge lake. You might choose to describe the campsite from the point of view of the night guards posted on a hill nearby or a village seen by Chuma and Wikatani as they approach through the jungle.

Hint: Remember to write from *one* character's "eyes," or point of view, using what that character sees, experiences, thinks, and feels to *show* rather than *tell* the story. (RESEARCH)

LIT/LA 10: Beauty is in the eye of the beholder—and so is danger! Imagine Chuma and Wikatani following the doctor into a strange village where, perhaps, no one had ever seen a white person before. What do Chuma and Wikatani see? What details do they notice? What are their thoughts and feelings? Write this scene from Chuma or Wikatani's point of view.

Now imagine you are a young man in this tribe. What do you see? What details do you notice? What are your thoughts and feelings? Write the same scene again, but from *this* boy's point of view. (WRITING)

LIT/LA 11: Choose an African folktale you enjoy. Create a puppet show using stick puppets to tell this story. You'll have to write the folktale as a script. Perhaps a narrator can tell the story as the characters speak their own lines. (DRAMA)

The Church Today

What is happening in the church today? Missionaries still tell about Jesus in places where his name has not been heard. Christian workers still bring food, medical care, and education to needy people. Christians around the globe still provide financial and prayer support to help this work.

CT 1: On page 94, the character Chuma prays, *"Oh, God...if you are the black man's God, too, as the doctor says, don't let him die."*

What was Chuma's understanding of God? What is the difference between God and gods? Across the world, people have often thought about God as Chuma did. Read Daniel 3. How did King Nebuchadnezzar understand God?

Read Ezra 1:1–4. What does the king say about God?

Read Mark 12:29 and Exodus 20:1–5. What does God say about himself?

Chuma and Wikatani did not know that one, true, living God had created the world. Were they bad people? Why did they understand God as they did? What did they need?

Read Romans 10:14–16. These, and other words like them, lit a fire in David Livingstone's heart to tell the people of Africa about the one, true, living God and his Son, Jesus.

In your best handwriting, write these verses from Romans on a card to post in a place where you will see it daily. Write these words on your hearts by memorizing them. (RESEARCH)

CT 2: Mission organizations including Frontiers, Wycliffe, Society for International Mission (SIM), and Youth With a Mission (YWAM) are some of the many mission organizations in Africa. Write or phone one organization for the name(s) of a missionary or missionary family. Ask for a photo of this person or family and a description of their work in Africa.

Post a map of Africa and this photo on the wall in a prominent place in your home or classroom. Mark the location of this missionary work with a colored pushpin.

Missionaries say they can tell when people are praying for them and when people forget. They report that when people pray, new Christians are baptized, people hear about Jesus, sick people get well, and the work seems easier. Without prayer support, mission work can seem like climbing an endless hill!

Pray every day for your missionary. On **Sunday**, pray that God will speak to this person or family and fill their hearts with love and praise for him.

Monday, pray that enough money will be given so the work can be done.

Tuesday, pray for the family members by name. Missionaries often miss family back home. Ask God to protect them from loneliness.

Wednesday, ask God to send people with hungry hearts who are ready to hear about Jesus.

Thursday, pray for new Christians. If your missionary or family works in a place where Christians are persecuted, pray for protection and courage for the Christians.

Friday, pray that God would keep your missionary friend(s) safe. Pray for safe travel, good health, and protection from evil spirits.

Saturday, pray for some rest, fun, friendship, and relaxation for your missionary friend(s). Ask God to bless and bless and bless them some more! (PRAY)

CT 3: How much do you think Chuma really understood when Dr. Livingstone baptized him? Do a survey of your neighborhood. Ask people what they think someone must *understand and believe* to be a Christian and what they think people must *do* to be a Christian.

Look at Scriptures like John 3:16; Romans 10:8–13, 3:23, and 6:23; Ephesians 2:8–9. Write what you might say to someone who has never even *heard* about Jesus or God. If you had only a short time, what "seeds" would you plant?

(*Note:* How often we Christians major on the minors! It is important to understand that even though we may see an area of sin in someone's life, God's plan is not to get them to shape up and get rid of the sin, then come to Jesus. Everything we must understand, believe, and do is about God's love shown to us in Jesus, even understanding that we need him because we sin.) (RESEARCH)

Resources

Titles in bold indicate resources particularly recommended for supplementing this Curriculum Guide.

Online: The following Internet Web sites are mentioned in this guide:

    http://dpsnet.detpub.k12.mi.us/heritage/gallery.htm

    http://memory.loc.gov/ammem/aap/timeline.html (timeline, photos)

    http://odur.let.rug.nl/~usa/D/1826-1850/slavery/fugit06

    http://scriptorium.lib.duke.edu/campbell/

    www.expediamaps.com

    www.lib.utexas.edu/Libs/PCL/Map_collection/africa

    www.loc.gov/exhibits/african/

    www.nationalgeographic.com/congotrek/

    www.nationalgeographic.com/features/99/railroad (timeline, artifacts)

    www.passporttoknowledge.com/rainforest

    www.raremaps.com

    www.sc.edu/library/spcoll/africa2.html (slavery: African history)

    www.sc.edu/library/spcoll/sccoll/africa/africa5.html

    www.trailblazerbooks.com (click on book cover)

    www.ugrr.org/ugrr (Underground Railroad)

Organizations:

    Frontiers: (800) GO 2 THEM

    Wycliffe: (800) WYCLIFFE

    Society for International Mission (SIM): (800) 521-6449

    Youth With a Mission (YWAM): (800) 992-2143

Print: The following resources are mentioned in this guide:

African Beginnings by James Haskins and Kathleen Benson. New York: Lothrop, Lee & Shepherd, 1998.

Africa's Trailblazer by Janet and Geoff Benge. Seattle: YWAM Publishers, 1999.[1]

Amistad: A Long Road to Freedom by Walter Dean Myers. New York: Dutton Children's Books, 1998.

Be a Friend: The Story of African American Music in Song, Words, and Pictures by Leotha Stanley: Madison, WI: Knowledge Unlimited Publishers.

The Captive by Joyce Hansen. New York: Scholastic, 1994.

Dear Friend: Thomas Garrett & William Still by Judith Bentley. New York, Cobblehill, 1997.

Escape From Slavery: Five Journeys to Freedom by Doreen Rappaport. New York: HarperCollins, 1991.

Escape From Slavery: The Boyhood of Frederick Douglass in His Own Words edited by Michael McCurdy. New York: Knopf, 1994.

Freedom's Sons: The True Story of the Amistad Mutiny by Suzanne Jurmain. New York: Lothrop, Lee & Shepherd, 1998.

From Slave Ship to Freedom Road by Julius Lester. New York: Dial Books, 1998.

Get on Board: The Story of the Underground Railroad by Jim Haskins. New York: Scholastic Publishers, 1993.

Harriet Beecher Stowe and the Beecher Preachers by Jean Fritz. New York: Putnam, 1994.

Incidents in the Life of a Slave Girl by Harriet Jacobs. New York: Harcourt, Brace, Jovanovich, 1973.

Listen for the Whippoorwill by Dave and Neta Jackson. Minneapolis: Bethany House, 1993.

Malawi by Martha S. B. Lane. Chicago: Children's Press, 1990.

Many Thousand Gone by Virginia Hamilton. New York, Knopf Publishers, 1993.

The Middle Passage by Tom Feelings. New York: Dial Books, 1995.

Mufaro's Beautiful Daughters by John

Steptoe. New York: Lothrop, Lee &
Shepherd, 1987.

My Name Is Not Angelica by Scott O'Dell.
New York: Dell, 1990.

National Geographic. Washington, D.C.:
National Graphic Society.[2]

One Day, Levin...He Be Free by Lurey
Khan. New York: E. P. Dutton, 1972.

Our Song, Our Toil by Michele Stepto.
Brookfield, CT: Millbrook Press, 1994.

The People Could Fly by Virginia Hamilton.
New York: Knopf, 1993.

People in Bondage by L. H. Ofosu. Minneapolis: Runestone Press, 1993.

*The Refugees: Narratives of Fugitive Slaves
in Canada* by Benjamin Drew. Boston:
Jewett, 1858. (Out of print but available
on interlibrary loan.)

Reminiscences of Levi Coffin by Levi Coffin.
Chicago: A. M. Kelley Publishers, 1968.

The Runaway's Revenge by Dave and Neta
Jackson. Minneapolis: Bethany House,
1995.

The Slave Dancer by Paula Fox. New York:
Dell, 1991.

The Underground Railroad by Charles
Blockson. New York: Berkley Books,
1994.

Walking the Road to Freedom by Jeri Ferris.
Minneapolis: CarolRhoda, 1988.

A Walk Through a Rain Forest by David
and Mark Jenike. New York: Franklin
Watts, 1995.

Why Mosquitoes Buzz in People's Ears by
Verna Aardema. New York: Penguin,
1992.

Video: The following resources are mentioned
in this guide:

Africa Close-up. Maryknoll Productions,
1997.[3]

Amistad, Dreamworks Producers, 1998.

Journey to 1,000 Rivers. Turner Home
Entertainment, 1987.

World's Greatest Places: Hidden Congo.
National Geographic Video, 1985.

---

[1] Youth With a Mission Publishers may be reached at (800) 922-2143.

[2] Articles and issues of *National Geographic* magazine listed in activity descriptions. Back issues:
(800) 647-5463. Education Dept: (800) 368-2728 for additional resources.

[3] Available from Mennonite Central Committee at (715) 859-1151 (U.S.) or (888) 622-6337 (Canada).